WANT TO SEE
THE CUTEST THING EVER?

IT'S A CUTE MONSTER!

OKAY, I GUESS IT COULD BE CUTER.

HOW ABOUT A CUTE MONSTER WITH . . .

A KITTEN!

OR MAYBE . . .

A MONSTER WITH TWO KITTENS!

AND WHAT iF BOTH THE
KITTENS WERE WEARiNG . . .

HOW ABOUT TWO KITTENS WEARING HATS . . .

INSIDE OF ANOTHER HAT!

THAT A CUTE MONSTER IS WEARING!

AND THEY'RE RIDING A UNICORN!!!

ISN'T IT
CUTE?

WAIT, COME BACK.
LOOK!

THEY'RE RIDING UP A
RAINBOW ROAD! YOU HAVE TO
ADMIT THAT IS CUTE, RIGHT?
ESPECIALLY IF THEY'RE BEING
FOLLOWED BY . . .

A PARADE OF KOALA BEARS!!!

LOOK, BUNNIES!

BUNNIES DRESSED LIKE . . .

BUNNY ASTRONAUTS!

A CUTE MONSTER WEARING
A HATFUL OF KITTENS WEARING HATS

RIDING A UNICORN THAT'S BEING
HUGGED BY KOALAS ON A RAINBOW ROAD

SURROUNDED BY ASTRONAUT BUNNIES
FLYING THROUGH SPACE!

ISN'T THAT THE CUTEST THING EVER?!!?

IT'S NOT?